For Julia and Abigail
—D. C.

For Doreen
—S. M.

Atheneum Books for Young Readers
An imprint of Simon & Schuster
Children's Publishing Division
1230 Avenue of the Americas
New York, New York 10020
Text copyright © 2007 by Doreen Cronin
Illustrations copyright © 2007
by Scott Menchin
Book design by Ann Bobco
The text for this book is set in Bliss.
The illustrations for this book are rendered
in pen and ink with digital color.
Manufactured in China
First Edition
1 2 3 4 5 6 7 8 9 10
Library of Congress
Cataloging-in-Publication Data
Cronin, Doreen.
Bounce / Doreen Cronin ;
illustrated by Scott Menchin—1st ed.
p.   cm.
Summary: Rhyming text offers advice
on the best ways for toddlers to bounce.
ISBN-13: 978-1-4169-1627-7
ISBN-10: 1-4169-1627-X
[1. Jumping—Fiction. 2. Toddlers—Fiction.
3. Stories in rhyme.]
I. Menchin, Scott, ill. II. Title.
PZ8.3.C879 Bou 2007
[E] 22—dc22   2005037128

BOUNCE
doreen cronin
scott menchin

atheneum books for young readers new york · london · toronto · sydney

C'mon!
Let's **bounce** like a bunny!

hip

hop

hip

hop

Let's
bounce
like
a frog!

ker- plop

I'll bounce to the left . . .

if you'll bounce to the **right.**

Bees
bounce
in
the
daytime.

Bats bounce in the night.

You can **bounce** a ball right off your **hands**

or bounce it off your toes.

I can
bounce a
beach ball
on the tip
of my
nose!

If you bounce into a **puddle,**

it's best to bounce in boots.

If you
must
bounce
in
the
market,

it's best **not** to bounce in fruits!

Bouncing
with your
best friend
is called a
bouncing
double.

Bouncing on the couch is called **big** bouncing **trouble.**

It's **hard** to bounce in roller skates,

it's **fun** to bounce on poles.

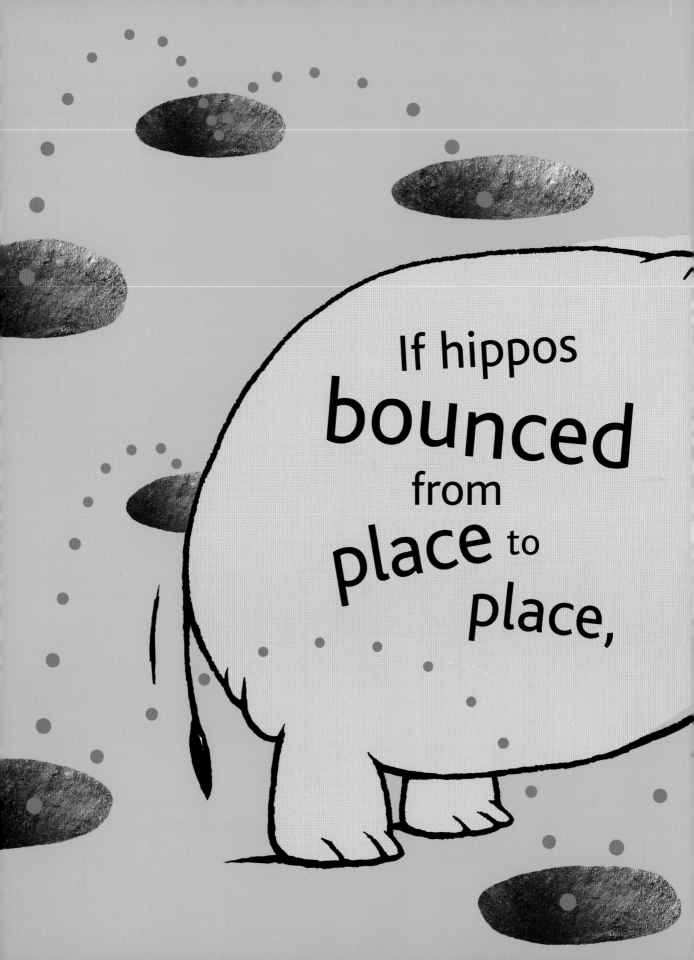

If hippos
bounced
from
place to
Place,

imagine all the holes!

bounce **back** into **the** shade.

If
bouncing
makes you
thirsty,

bounce
yourself
to lemonade.

A bounce can turn into a bump,

a bump into a fall.

But it's better to have **bounced** and **bumped** ...

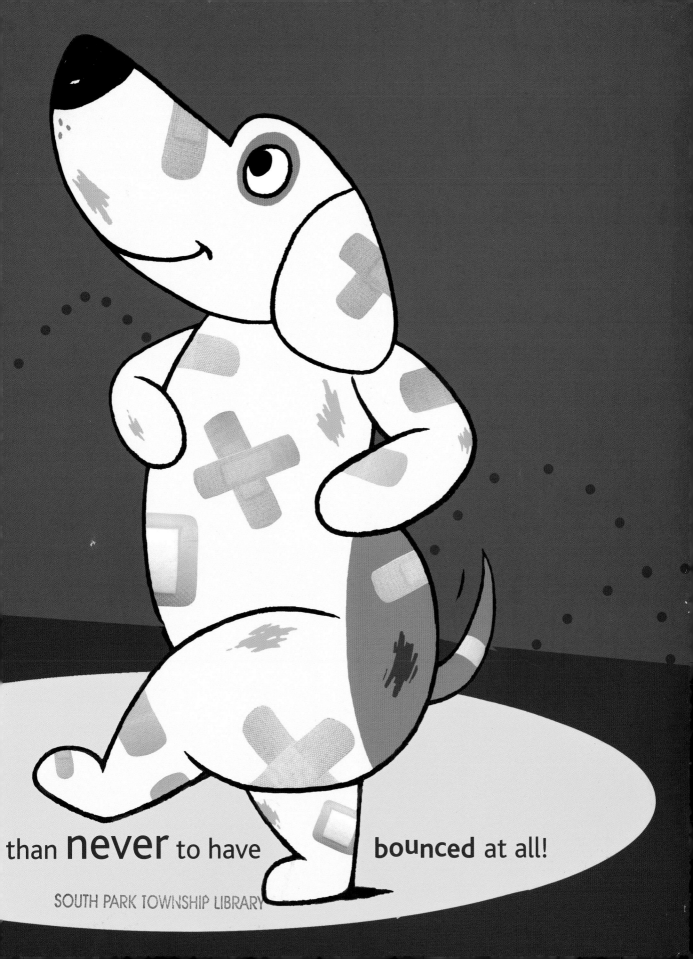

than **never** to have **bounced** at all!